Dear Josephine, Oliver, + Lilah,

May you always believe in kindness!

Love, Stephanie
+ Beatrice

Praise for *Beatrice and the Sunflower Gift*

"*Beatrice and the Sunflower Gift* is a truly insightful and inspiring children's book set in a garden meadow. It is a lovely tale of a shy, selfless turtle who learns to come out of her shell by giving to others. Her caring spirit uplifts all the animals in the forest."

—Dr. Elizabeth Cappella, Distinguished Service Professor, SUNY

"In *Beatrice and the Sunflower Gift*, a young, small turtle leaves a sunflower for a young bunny, a mama robin, and a sleeping bear in hopes that these gifts would brighten their day. Little did Beatrice know that her act of kindness would multiply a thousand-fold."

—Dr. Geraldine Bard, Professor of English, Emeritus, SUNY

"In the pages of *Beatrice and the Sunflower Gift*, you'll find a delightful story of Beatrice finding her way into discovering the beauty of friendships. All children will enjoy the lesson of making new friends, especially for a child seeking to build comfort and confidence in this challenging process."

—Dave Bauer, Author, *What's Under That Rock, Papa?*

"Emboldened by the warm embrace of a butterfly and robin, Beatrice, a timid turtle, tiptoes out of her comfort zone to experience beauty and goodness beyond her protective shell. *Beatrice and the Sunflower Gift* gently inspires young readers to be courageous; to choose curiosity over fear, and friendship over solitude. A celebration of kindness, *Beatrice and the Sunflower Gift* encourages readers to think of others and act accordingly. Kindness is contagious."

—M.T. DiVencenzo

"Parwulski's story of a shy little turtle shows the importance of even the smallest acts of kindness. Beatrice's desire to share the beauty of nature prompts her to reach out bravely to others, leading to unexpected new friendships. Even the most timid young reader will be inspired and encouraged by her experiences."

—Nancy Marck Cantwell, Ph.D.

ISBN: 978-1-947860-05-6

LCCN: 2018932694

Printed in the United States

Published by

BELLE ISLE BOOKS

www.belleislebooks.com

Beatrice
—AND THE SUNFLOWER GIFT—

Written by Stephanie Parwulski

Illustrated by Tania Ramírez Cuevas

For my mom,
my angel in Heaven,
whose radiant light
still shines so bright

Acknowledgments

To my supportive team, I send my heartfelt gratitude to each one of you:

My dad, thank you for always encouraging my dreams and lifting me up with your unconditional love.

My brother, Stephen, thank you for believing in my manuscript and encouraging me to send it to a publisher. I could not have done this without you!

My grandparents, thank you for guiding me with your wisdom and care, like Donna the Robin does for Beatrice the Turtle.

My aunts, uncles, and cousins, thank you for continually cheering me on.

My friends, Grace, Daniel, Courtney, Sue, Rachel, Meghan, and Maddie, thank you for always being there for me and standing by me at every step of this meaningful journey.

My colleagues, Dave and Michaelene, thank you for giving me the opportunities to grow and for believing in my potential.

My mentors, Dr. Bard, Dr. Cappella, Maria T. DiVencenzo, and KarenMarie, thank you for encouraging me to be open to life's endless possibilities and for broadening my horizons.

My teachers from the Clarence schools and my professors from Daemen College, thank you for nurturing my love of reading and writing and giving me the confidence to pursue my dreams.

My publishing team, thank you for making my book a reality. My illustrator, Tania, thank you for bringing my vision of Beatrice to life. This truly is a dream come true, and I love working with all of you!

My readers, thank you for supporting me! You are an important part of my journey as an author, and I hope that through my writing, you find inspiration and encouragement.

Beatrice the Turtle lived in a rock garden on the edge of a small pond. She often did not come out of her shell, so most other animals thought she was a rock, too.

Beatrice liked to stay in her shell because she was afraid of the big world. *I'm so small,* she thought. *What if the other animals don't like me? I'm much safer in my comforting shell.*

One summer day, a little white butterfly landed on a rock in front of Beatrice. Slowly poking her head out of her shell, Beatrice wondered where the butterfly had come from.

As Beatrice followed the butterfly, she noticed many beautiful things all around her.

First, Beatrice saw a peaceful waterfall that was small, like her. The water splashed over the rocks and sprayed Beatrice, refreshing her and making her giggle with delight.

Second, Beatrice visited the Tree Grove. She stood in the center of this circle of tall trees and looked up in amazement. Their branches almost touched the sky!

Third, Beatrice stopped at a patch of dandelions. As the wind blew, feathery seeds from the dandelions separated from their stems, and it looked like they were dancing. Just like the wind, Beatrice blew on a dandelion and watched its seeds twirl in the air.

As Beatrice thought about all of the wonderful places the butterfly had shown her, she noticed that the world seemed more inviting. She was not so afraid anymore.

The butterfly finally landed on a yellow petal in a sunflower field.

The sunflowers were so pretty, glowing in the sunlight. Beatrice decided to take some with her for her homeward journey.

Beatrice was thankful that the butterfly had not left her, because she was not sure of the way back to her rock garden.

On the way home, the butterfly led Beatrice to a meadow, where a bunny practiced hopping. The bunny was so focused on hopping high in the air that she did not notice Beatrice. Beatrice was too nervous to cheer the bunny on, so she left a sunflower for encouragement.

The butterfly took flight again and then rested near a small pine tree. Beatrice noticed a mama robin and her little ones in a nest inside the tree. The mama robin was feeding small berries to her three babies. The young robins caught the food that the mama robin dropped for them. Beatrice did not want to interrupt, so she left a sunflower at the base of the tree to show her appreciation of the mama robin's love and care for her children.

Then, the butterfly landed at the opening of a bear's den. Beatrice was a little scared because the bear was so much bigger than she was. However, the bear was sleeping and seemed friendly and gentle. Beatrice left a sunflower for the bear, too, thinking it would be a nice surprise when he woke up.

The butterfly finally brought Beatrice home. As Beatrice put the last sunflower from her journey beside her rock bed, the butterfly disappeared. She looked in every direction but could not find it. Beatrice would miss the butterfly, yet she was happy it was on a new journey to brighten someone else's day.

Beatrice was grateful for all the butterfly had shown her of the great, big world beyond her rock garden.

"Thank you, little butterfly!" Beatrice whispered toward the sky.

Back in the forest, the other animals discovered their sunflowers, and a smile was brought to each of their faces.

That was very kind,
thought Lee the Bunny.

What a beautiful gift!
thought Donna the Robin.

*How sweet of someone
to think of me!*
thought Mack the Bear.

As Lee, Donna, and Mack looked at their sunflowers, they were reminded of the beautiful sunflower field at the forest's edge. They each decided to visit it and were pleasantly surprised when they all arrived at the same time.

"Hi, Lee! Hi, Donna! Did you also receive a sunflower today?" Mack asked.

"Yes!" said Donna. "Let's spread more happiness by delivering sunflowers to the rest of our forest friends."

"That's a great idea!" Lee said.

For the rest of the afternoon, Lee, Donna, and Mack journeyed in different directions throughout the forest, gifting others with the sunflowers they picked. All of the animals were appreciative of the sunflower gift they received.

At the end of the day, the animals came together at the Tree Grove, bringing their sunflowers with them. They were all so happy and wanted to rejoice in each other's friendship.

As Donna the Robin flew overhead, making sure everybody had been invited, she noticed a lonesome sunflower in a rock garden. She landed on a rock and called, "Hello? Is anyone here?"

Suddenly, the rock beneath Donna's feet moved. *This isn't a rock!* thought Donna. *This is a turtle!*

Donna flew off of the turtle's shell and perched on a nearby rock. Beatrice poked her head out of her shell and saw the mama robin standing in front of her. "I'm sorry to have frightened you, little one. What is your name?" Donna the Robin asked.

Beatrice said in a soft voice, "My name is Beatrice."

Donna the Robin smiled and said, "It's very nice to meet you, Beatrice. My name is Donna. I was wondering if you wanted to come to the Tree Grove with me. The other animals of the forest are there, too. Someone gave us sunflowers today, and we want to celebrate that act of kindness. I see you also received a sunflower!"

Beatrice smiled. She was glad her sunflowers had brought everyone together. However, she felt nervous about the invitation. "I'm really shy," Beatrice said. "That's why I usually stay inside my shell."

Donna nodded. "You don't have to worry, sweetheart. I'll stay right beside you. You already have a friend in me."

Beatrice smiled and followed Donna's lead, bringing her sunflower with her. Just like the butterfly, Donna comforted Beatrice. Beatrice was grateful for Donna's company.

When Beatrice and Donna arrived at the Tree Grove, Beatrice was amazed by what she saw. All of the forest animals had their sunflowers with them, creating a sea of yellow and brown.

"Hi, everyone!" Donna said. "This is my new friend, Beatrice!" Beatrice was ready to retreat into her shell, but stopped herself when the other animals replied, "Hi, Beatrice! We welcome you to our celebration of friendship."

The animals introduced themselves to Beatrice, who recognized Lee the Bunny and Mack the Bear. As she spoke to the other animals, Beatrice discovered an inner sense of courage that she hadn't previously felt. It was a comfort to Beatrice that, as promised, Donna stayed by her side.

Some of the animals began asking who had originally delivered the sunflowers. Beatrice smiled to herself and chose not to answer. She was just happy to bring joy to others.

The greatest gift Beatrice could ever receive was friendship, and with each sunflower came a new friend!

ABOUT THE AUTHOR

Stephanie Parwulski firmly believes that when words are used positively, they have the power to touch others deeply. Because of her lifelong love of children's literature, Stephanie is excited for her authorial debut. *Beatrice and the Sunflower Gift* is her first children's book, and she looks forward to writing more! Stephanie gathers inspiration from reading, singing, and gardening. She enjoys spending time with her family and friends and going on adventures. Stephanie lives in Buffalo, NY, working as a preschool aide and writing mental health articles for "The Mighty."

ABOUT THE ILLUSTRATOR

Tania Ramírez Cuevas is an illustrator born in Mérida Yucatán, México. She studied for a degree in graphic design in her hometown, and after a year of working as a graphic designer she decided to be a professional illustrator since her passion has always been drawing. Working mostly as a freelance illustrator, Tania specializes in children's illustration, cartoon, character design and webcomics. She has her own webcomic called "Un Gato en la Ciudad" ("A Cat in the City"), where she shares her personal experiences and views of life in the cities of México. Tania has also worked giving conferences and drawing classes for teenagers and adults.

CPSIA information can be obtained
at www.ICGtesting.com
Printed in the USA
BVHW02*0533210818
524665BV00005B/7/P